Here Comes SANTA!

by Molly Wigand
illustrated by Ed Resto

Simon Spotlight/Nickelodeon

KLASKY CSUPO INC.

Based on the TV series *Rugrats*® created by Arlene Klasky, Gabor Csupo, and
Paul Germain as seen on Nickelodeon®

SIMON SPOTLIGHT
An imprint of Simon & Schuster Children's Publishing Division
1230 Avenue of the Americas
New York, New York 10020

First Edition
2 4 6 8 10 9 7 5 3 1

ISBN 0-689-82571-4

Busy shoppers hurried through the mall. Loud music blared. Store windows sparkled with toys and decorations.

"I love Christmas!" whispered Tommy. "Just look at all the toys!"

"Listen to the music!" Susie cried.

"Listen to *my* music," said Angelica. "We witch you a scary kiss-moose, we witch you a scary kiss-moose!" she sang off-key.

"I don't like the sound of that," whispered Chuckie.

"Aw, Chuckie. Don't worry," Phil replied softly.

Chuckie's dad, Chas, pointed to the mall's lower level. "Look, Chuckie!" he said. "Santa's right down there." Chuckie covered his eyes with his mittens.

"Don't worry," said Chas. "Santa is a friend to children everywhere!"

Angelica leaned down to Chuckie. "Santa's no friend," she said. "He's a big, fat elf with a scratchy beard who runs around in red pajamas."

"What's wrong with red pajamas?" whispered Tommy.

"Are you kids ready?" Didi asked.

Angelica whispered to the babies, "Are you ready for the scare of your little baby lives?"

"What do you mean, *scare*, Angelica?" whispered Chuckie.

"Don't you know? Santa is one spooky guy," she replied. "And don't let that 'Ho-Ho-Ho' stuff fool you. He's just waiting for dumb babies like you to mess up so he can put you on his bad kid list."

"Are you sure?" Chuckie asked.

"Yeah," Angelica said. "And you know what else? He smells like a reindeer. But that's not the worst thing!"

"W-w-what's the worst thing?" asked Chuckie.

"He lands on your roof in the middle of the night. You might even hear him stomping around," Angelica warned.

"She's just trying to scare you," Tommy said, patting Chuckie's arm.

"She's doing a pretty good job," said Chuckie.

"Come on, guys," said Betty. "Let's ride the escalator."

Chuckie's eyes got very big. "We gotta ride an alligator?" he asked, his voice trembling.

"Not an alligator." Angelica snorted. "An escalator! Don't you know anything?"

The brave mommies and Chas picked up the babies and stepped onto the escalator. The moving steps carried everyone down to Santa's Wonderland. When the babies got off, Tommy watched lines of people going up and down.

"You know what?" Tommy giggled. "I think I like escalators."

"Yeah," said Phil. "Maybe we'll like Santa, too!"

"Are we there yet?" asked Chuckie with his eyes squeezed shut.

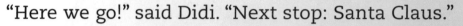

"Here we go!" said Didi. "Next stop: Santa Claus."

Dozens of elves scurried through the Wonderland, pushing children toward Santa's castle.

Just then a loud voice boomed all through the mall. "Attention, Christmas shoppers! The first shipment of Space Shuttle Cynthia dolls has just arrived at Santa's Workshop. Come and see this season's hottest new toy!"

"I gotta have one of those dolls!" Angelica exclaimed. "See you babies later!"

"But, Angelica!" said Tommy. "You'll miss Santa!"

"Big deal!" Angelica called over her shoulder as she rushed away.

Angelica dashed
toward the giant Cynthia.
"Outta my way!" she hollered,
climbing over children and up to the top
of the space shuttle display. "These toys are
going to be mine. All mine!"

Meanwhile the line in Santa's Wonderland moved very slowly.
"I didn't think the North Pole would be so hot," Tommy said.
"I hope all these pretty snow-fakes don't melt," said Phil.
Baby Dil started to cry.
"Poor Dil," said Chuckie. "I bet he hates that warm snowsuit."
"It's okay, little brother," said Tommy as he unzipped the tiny snowsuit.
"Here, Dil," said Susie. "Have a lick of my candy cane."
Baby Dil stopped crying. He started to smile. Then he giggled and clapped his hands.

Pretty soon the babies could see the top of Santa's big red chair.

"Listen, kids," said Chas. "Can you hear good old Santa Claus?"

"Ho! Ho! Ho!" said a loud, deep voice.

"No! No! No!" whispered Chuckie.

"Aw, come on, Chuckie," said Tommy. "How scary can he be? He's just an elf!"

"He's got a pretty loud voice for an elf," Chuckie replied.

The babies rounded the last corner of the line. They saw Santa sitting in his huge red chair.

"He's kind of big for an elf," whispered Chuckie.

Didi carried Baby Dil to Santa's chair.

"That poor kid," Chuckie moaned.

"Hey, look!" said Tommy. "Dil's pulling Santa's beard."

Santa's beard was soft and fuzzy. Baby Dil giggled out loud.

Chas gently led Chuckie to Santa. "Now it's your turn," Chas said.

"You too, Tommy!" said Didi. "Phil, Lil, and Susie, go on up. There's room for everyone! Angelica too."

Santa helped the babies onto his big soft lap.

"You children were nice to Baby Dil," Santa said, giving each of the kids a reindeer hat.

"Hey, Tommy!" whispered Chuckie. "Santa doesn't smell like a reindeer!"

"I know," giggled Tommy. "He smells like cookies and milk!"

"Oh, no! Where's Angelica?" asked Chas.

Suddenly the loud voice spoke again. "We have a lost little girl in Santa's Wonderland. Her name is—"

"Angelica!" yelled Didi and Chas. They grabbed the babies from Santa's lap and ran to the giant space shuttle display. The grown-ups found Angelica buried in a pile of Cynthia dolls.

"How did you get lost?" Didi asked.

"I wasn't lost." Angelica pouted. "I was just looking at Space Shuttle Cynthia. Can I have one? Please?"

"Maybe Santa will bring you that toy, Angelica," said Didi.

Angelica's eyes lit up. "I've got to go ask him. And I've got to ask him for the Cynthia sleeping bag, and the Cynthia princess castle, and the Cynthia sports car . . ."

"I'm sorry, Angelica," said Didi. "But when you ran away from us, you missed your turn to see Santa."

Angelica burst into tears. Didi put her arm around her to comfort her.

"Hey, I know what'll cheer Angelica up," said Betty. "Let's go get some hot cocoa!"

"Great idea!" exclaimed Didi as they all headed toward Mrs. Claus's Cookie Kitchen.

"Ho! Ho! Ho!" said a familiar voice. "Look who's here."

Santa was taking a break.

Santa looked straight at Angelica. "You must be Angelica," he said. "I heard you ran away from these grown-ups without permission."

Angelica saw her chance.

"I'm really sorry," she said sweetly. "Do you think you could still bring me Space Shuttle Cynthia? Even though I messed up a weensy teensy tiny little bit today?"

Phil nudged Chuckie and whispered, "I thought she said he stunk like a reindeer!"

"Hmm . . ." said Santa. "Maybe you really don't want me to come to your house?"

"Uh-oh!" said Angelica, turning red.

Santa smiled. "Do you promise to behave and listen to these grown-ups?" he asked.

"I promise," Angelica said. "Floss my heart!"

"Ho! Ho! Ho! Then I'll see what I can do!" said Santa. "But now would you help Santa do something special?"

"Okay!" exclaimed Angelica.

Santa led the babies to a little room behind Santa's Workshop where one tiny reindeer munched on carrots and hay.

"Isn't he adorable!" exclaimed Didi.

"How would you children like to help me feed my reindeer?" Santa asked, his eyes twinkling.

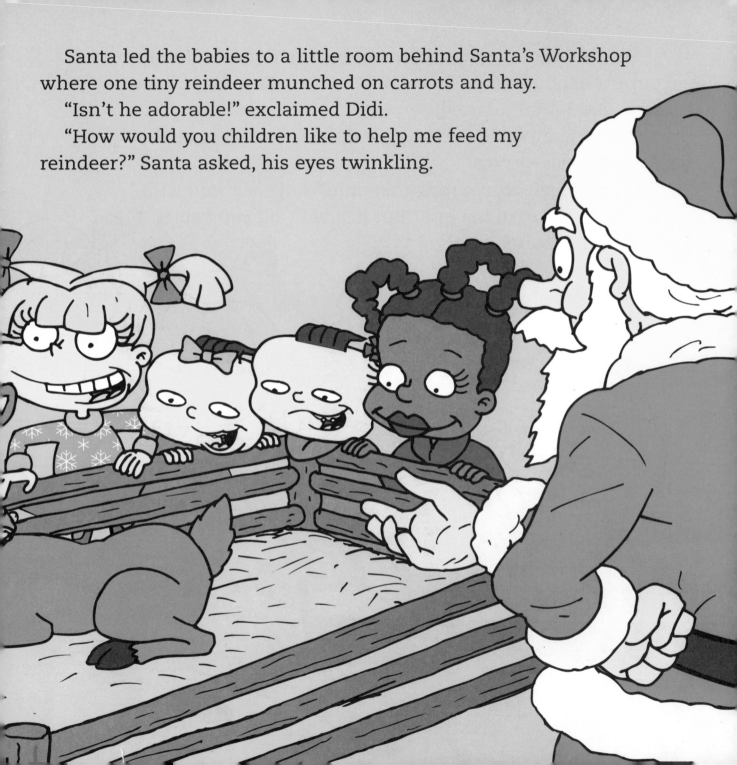

As the children gave carrots to Santa's reindeer, Tommy put his hand on Chuckie's shoulder. "See, Chuckie? I knew we'd like Santa!" he said.

"Yeah, Tommy!" Chuckie agreed. "He's not scary at all. Angelica was wrong!"

"I may have been wrong this time," Angelica said with a sneaky gleam in her eye. "But just wait till you babies meet the Easter Bunny!"